Prai

"Lives interwoven and cookies that arrive too late. This bravura collection of linked stories provides a profound lesson in empathy, of pouring yourself into someone else's life, someone else's pain, to see it from the inside, looking out."

Will Ferguson
Giller-winning author of *419*

"Flash fiction made more powerful with the linkage of cookies, prevalent in each captivating scene, it made me feel like I was sitting across the table from an old friend dining on cookies and village gossip. A story of forgiveness, acceptance, and relationships, *The Price of Cookies* offers flavour for every palate."

Miramichi Reader **(Sarah Butland)**

"The brief stories contained here fire like prisms, shining a welcome light into our collective darkness. These linked passages will tear at you, while simultaneously applying empathy and healing. Here find an artfully detailed small town and its lives effortlessly crafted to represent our world entire. We are very lucky to have Burnett."

Michael Blouin
2x winner ReLit Award for Best Novel

"*The Price of Cookies* reveals the price of a great many things: of grief, of love and desire, of heartbreak and indifference, of small joys and great loss. Finnian Burnett's novella ... is at once tragic and funny, alive with the full spectrum of human emotion and all the many ways we might be with one another: as lovers, friends, companions, kind strangers or cruel ones, curious neighbours and hopeful parents. ... As we've come to expect from Burnett, *The Price of Cookies* is both fantastic storytelling and insightful observation on the human condition–and a joy to read."

Christina Myers
award-winning author of
The List of Last Chances
and *Halfway Home*

"Burnett's ability to weave together these short flash fiction stories, combining common threads of loss, grief, and acceptance, is a wonder to behold. *The Price of Cookies* is a beautifully shared learning experience seen from the perspective of characters who feel like family. Take these stories a bite at a time and keep coming back for more!"

Andrew Buckley
Death, the Devil, and the Goldfish

"I can't believe how fast I read this book. Each story is artfully woven with the next; what at first seems like a compendium of short stories becomes an entire town of people looking out for each other, striving to do what is right, and dealing with their pain. Burnett's turn of phrase brings close the tension between desire for community and fear of judgement, all anchored by the universal comfort of a cookie. You won't be able to put it down."

Veronica Kirin
author of *Stories of Elders,*
cofounder of *Anodyne Magazine*

Praise for Finnian Burnett

"This interweaving of form and content is reminiscent of Margaret Atwood's craft."
Blank Spaces

"A gut-punch. Absolutely terrific!"
Robert J. Sawyer
Hugo and Nebula-winning author of
The Terminal Experiment

"More real than breath — which it truly takes away."
Pulp Literature

"A story that examines external and internal truths."
Bath Flash Fiction Award 2022, Michelle Elvy

"Empathetic and compassionate."
K.A. Mielke
author of *Victory Lap*

The Price of Cookies

by Finnian Burnett

Off Topic Publishing

First print edition: May 2024 by Off Topic Publishing

Copyright © Finnian Burnett, 2024

All rights reserved. No part of this publication may be reproduced, stored or transmitted in any form or by any means, electronic, mechanical, photocopying, recording, scanning, or otherwise without written permission from the publisher. It is illegal to copy this book, post it to a website, or distribute it by any other means without written permission, except for brief passages quoted in a review.

NO AI TRAINING: Without in any way limiting the author's and the publisher's exclusive rights under copyright, any use of this publication to "train" generative artificial intelligence (AI) technologies to generate text is expressly prohibited. The author reserves all rights to license uses of this work for generative AI training and development of machine learning language models.

Paperback ISBN: 978-1-7389885-2-5

eBook ISBN: 978-1-7389885-3-2

Edited by Marion Lougheed

Cover Design: Shannon Calcott

Off Topic Publishing: www.offtopicpublishing.com

This book is a work of fiction. Names, characters, places and incidents are either a product of the author's imagination or are used fictitiously. Any resemblance to actual people living or dead, events or locales is entirely coincidental.

To Lord Gordo, the Magnificent,

my purr-tner in crime,

who came into my life in 2014

and left it in 2023.

Contents

The Price of Cookies 1

The Cookies Adam Can't Eat 4

The Taste of Grief 7

In the Principal's Office 11

Mrs. Stanley's Smile 14

John Stanley Fixes Things 17

The Town Bakery 19

Sparrows Mate for Life 22

Painting the Walls of Raj's Tiny Room 25

Principal of the Year 27

Always Hungry 30

Mr. Leopold Goes for a Run 34

Alistair's Teacher 36

My Mother's Fingers 39

Mrs. Leopold's Cookies 41

A Pocketful of Cookies 44

Adam at the Table 45

Free Cookies Taste Better 47

Better than Homemade 50

At Adam's House 53

This Girl 57

Cigarettes and a Flowered Housedress 59

My Sister's Life 64

Kelvin Comes Home 66

The Feather He Brings 71

Back in the Bakery 73

Acknowledgements 77

Bonus Content 79

    A Note From Finnian 81

    My Office Window 83

    The Day the Ants Took Over Forever....... 84

    Denture Man and Hot Dog Mo 86

Kanga Catches a Break 89

Wolf and the Redhead.............................. 91

Great-Great-Grandpa's Teeth 93

Mannequin Body Parts 95

Francis Becomes Disillusioned at Rodeo-Clown School 98

About the Author 101

More Books from Off Topic Publishing............ 103

The Price of Cookies

The boy wandered the aisles of the shop and the clerk watched. She didn't watch closely; her feet hurt after seven hours on shift, and she didn't want to go to the trouble of leaving the counter. But she watched as he moved in and out of view and she saw the moment when he slipped the cookies—oatmeal raisin—into his pocket.

The boy's hollow cheeks, the dark circles under his eyes and the hand-me-down clothes that hung from his slender frame gave him a waifish appearance. The clerk wanted to give him the cookies, pay for them herself, offer an apple maybe or a granola bar to go along with them. He looked kind of like her Bobby before he enlisted, all knees and elbows. A kid like that needed more to eat than cookies.

But the security cameras might have seen the cookie theft and it wasn't worth the clerk's job to let a kid, even a hungry-looking kid like that, walk away with a buck ninety-nine worth of stolen merchandise.

The boy approached the counter and veered to the left, waving a hand at the clerk with what he hoped was an air of *Just looking, didn't find what I wanted*, but the clerk called him back and instead of running, the boy, whose name was Kelvin, emptied his pockets onto the counter, unearthing a wallet containing a brand-new driver's licence, a folded piece of paper, a pocketknife, a cool rock he'd found in the park earlier, and the package of cookies he'd shoved into his coat in aisle three, though he wasn't even hungry.

They both shifted uncomfortably—Kelvin debating whether there was still time to grab his things and run—the clerk debating whether it was worth the pay she made at this job to deal with trying to have a hungry teenager arrested.

They stared at each other for a few moments.

Neither knew the other was hanging on just this side of crying.

The clerk sighed, shoved everything back across the counter and said, "Don't come back here."

Kelvin left, knowing he'd have to find a new store, further away, leaving his mother longer than he wanted. And he walked back through the park, back to the hospital. He tried to eat one of the cookies, but he could barely choke it down his throat.

The Cookies Adam Can't Eat

Bobby can still feel the squelchy bits of his best friend's intestines sliding down his face. He had scrubbed until it was as raw as Lady Macbeth's hands and he can still feel them oozing across his cheek, dripping onto his uniform.

A routine patrol. Adam's face, smiling back at Bobby, his left eye dropped in an exaggerated wink. *Nothing to worry about, buddy. Stop being such an old lady.*

Scrubbing his face again. Adam's torso and head pieced back together for the trip home. *Go see my wife*, Adam said. *If anything happens.* Bobby promised but he knew he wouldn't, though she lived so close he could almost walk there. *His guts dripped down my face*, Bobby would tell Adam's son and the newly bereaved widow. Adam's wife would serve him cookies; Adam always raved about his wife's cookies. *You'll see*, Adam said. He waited at mail call every day. *Someday you'll taste these cookies, and you'll realize you've never tasted homemade cookies before.*

Adam's wife would make cookies and serve them to Bobby. They'd taste so good; he'd forget to wash his face. *Tell me about Adam*, she might say, and Bobby would tell her how Adam never made fun of his stutter, how Adam told the other guys to lay off and the other guys always did. *He loved you*, he'd say. *His eyes, they did this thing when he talked about you.*

Adam and his wife lived close to Bobby's hometown. They may have even run into each other, Adam once said, at the comic store in the town between their two homes. Might have seen each other more than once, even.

Bobby dunks his face in the plugged sink, lathering himself until his skin burns and the towel scrapes over his cheeks like sandpaper.

You got a girl? Adam once asked. Bobby didn't.

He just had his mom, and she didn't bake cookies, didn't have time. *You got a guy then?* Adam, smiling because it didn't matter. Friends for life. What happened back home didn't exist.

Mail call. Someone throws a box on his bed. Curling, feminine handwriting addressed to Bobby. Cinnamon and chocolate wafts from the paper. Bobby's fingers trace the letters of his own name, trace the grease spots starting to shine through the brown wrapping paper. *You'll see*, Adam had said. *Someday.* Bobby's hands shred the paper and reach for a fistful of cookies, shoving them against his lips. *Someday*, Adam said. *Someday.* Bobby's hands move automatically, his throat dry-swallows the cookies, handful by handful. Tears burn down his raw cheeks and mix with the cookie shards on his lips. He eats until he's sick, eats until he can't swallow. He's still eating when the medics come for him, still grasping for handfuls as they carry him away.

The Taste of Grief

Your first mistake is thinking grief is sadness. Grief swallows you, sucks you into a quicksand of numbness. The world blurs into slashes of red and purple, that enrage and comfort you all at once. *He died on a routine patrol*, they said. The words attack you from a distance, just like your best friend's hand, your child's cries, the aroma of fresh-baked cookies you meant to send him a dozen times over the past year but there was always something else to do, an errand to run, a school play to attend or you were out of butter and by the time you got to the store and picked up the laundry soap and snack packs for the boy's lunch and a roasted chicken because you knew you wouldn't have time to make dinner, you forgot why you were there in the first place.

Flowers, a crush of bodies, hands, people groping for you with their wet faces and sombre voices. *So young, so sad, so sudden.* Your best friend stands beside you with your son at her side. The minister's wife wears thick-soled beige loafers; her stockings pool around her ankles and you want to rip them from her legs, cursing the high-heeled black shoes scraping blisters into your pinkie toes.

A voice, insistent and panicked, invades your drugged sleep. *Where are the cookies?* The roar in your head obfuscates the source until you catch a flash of golden curls. It's Adam. *Where are the cookies? You promised you'd send them.* He's so angry, so unlike your real-life Adam, with his big, goofy grin and that unruly shock of curly hair, the hair your son inherited, hair that can't be tamed no matter how many times you take him to the barber. *Where are the cookies? You promised.*

You're creaming butter and sugar, mixing flour, baking soda, a touch of vanilla. Frenzied, you slap the dough onto the counter and slam the rolling pin against it. If you can just make enough, if you can just make yourself package them and take them to the post office. *It's 2 AM, sweetie, what are you doing?* Your best friend's compassionate voice fuels your anger. She stands there, holding your son's hand as if protecting him from you. He reaches for a cookie, and you snap, throwing a wooden spoon at him. *They're for your father.*

Your knees go weak, and you collapse on the kitchen floor. The boy drops next to you, his golden curls coated with cookie dough. *Mom, please.*

Your arms curl around him, an automatic response to a child's distress but even as you're holding him, you know you're not there and when you're both standing again and the child reaches for a cookie to take with him back to bed, you slap his hand away and push him out of the room.

Your best friend, who has been staying with you since you heard, wraps her arms around your shoulders as you turn back to your baking. *All the cookies in the world won't bring him back*, she says in your ear.

I know, you tell her. *I know.* But you don't know it, not really, and before she's even back in bed you're already mixing another batch of dough.

In the Principal's Office

Josh sat in the main office, staring at the principal's closed door. He knew his mother was in there because he could smell her Estée Lauder, the brown stuff in a bottle his dad bought her every year for Christmas until the last one.

Josh could feel the secretary's eyes on him, feel her fake sympathy. "Lost his father," he overheard her say to the teacher standing near her desk.

The principal's door opened and Mr. Farber motioned Josh into the room. As he entered, his mother's disappointed eyes tracked over and past him. Her frown made the wrinkles on her face stand out and the idea that she was old hit Josh. He wanted to reach for her, to hold her in this moment. Instead, he sat and faced Mr. Farber, who said, "We just want to talk about why you stole Mrs. Eaton's cookies."

"Mom," Josh said. He just wanted her to look

at him, to acknowledge him. Even when her eyes met his, they were far away, not with him, never with him. Mrs. Eaton's homemade cookies, wrapped in a wad of paper towels from the boy's bathroom, weighed down his pocket and he reached for them, tossing the whole crumbled mess on the desk. Mr. Farber stared at it over his glasses. "I'm here to help, Josh. I'm not the enemy."

Expel me, Josh wanted to say, but he sat silently. Mr. Farber handed a business card across the desk to Josh's mom. "We're not interested in punishing him," he said. "But I do wish the two of you would consider family counselling." He reached across the desk and patted Josh's hand. His face was compassionate, but Josh knew his mother would never take him to counselling. It was easier for her to stay trapped in her own pain than it was to deal with Josh's.

Josh's mother stood and Mr. Farber ushered

her out of the office. As Josh stood to follow, Mr. Farber's Principal of the Year trophy caught his eye. As his mother said goodbye to the principal, Josh's hands reached out. He hefted the trophy and hurled it through the office window.

Mrs. Stanley's Smile

Mrs. Stanley's fingers rifle through the file cabinet. M. N. O. P. Parker. She cocks her head, listening for Mr. Farber's footsteps. Silence. She pulls the folder and opens it, scanning the page. Fighting in the hall. Late to class. Failure to report to detention. The Parker boy has been in consistent trouble since his father died. She wishes John had died instead of leaving her for the man who runs the bakery on Eighth Street where she used to buy snickerdoodles three times a week until she found out the man was fucking her husband.

Mrs. Stanley notices the mother's unlaundered clothing and unkempt nails when she comes in to talk to Mr. Farber about her troubled son again and again. No one knows that Mrs. Stanley's husband is a homosexual now or that he's living in a studio apartment above the bakery with the man who used to whistle classical music while he packed her cookies and tell her how beautiful she looked in her new orange sweater set.

Mrs. Stanley still smiles at everyone who enters the office, even when she's screaming inside, even when she wants to jump over the counter and shake them, accost them with questions. *How do you keep living? How do you keep waking up every morning when there's nothing left?* She imagines herself with wild hair like the mother, a mustard stain on her skirt, dark circles under her eyes, gripping the gym teacher's collar and shrieking, *How do you make it make sense?*

The Parker boy's mother doesn't wear makeup anymore. Mrs. Stanley carefully applies her own face every day while Mr. Bellyjangles purrs next to her on the vanity, staring up at her with the adoration her husband failed to show her in the seventeen years they'd been tethered.

The mother shuffles out of Mr. Farber's office.

Mrs. Stanley wants to take her to the salon, to fix the dark roots that have been growing out for far too long. *It gets better*, she doesn't say. *You learn to live with it.* Her hands itch to touch the mother, to wrap her into a hug, to say, *At least he still loved you when he died, at least he still did.* But she smiles as the mother creeps past and says instead, *See you next time.*

John Stanley Fixes Things

His face is soft, like his mouth, his words. Long fingers knead the dough every morning, the strong muscles of his forearms flexing as he flips, pushes, slaps. I come for coffee—he opens early so I can get a cup before I open the shop. He sings and hums while he works, and the sound washes over me as warmly as the steam from my cup and the yeasty scent of fresh bread. He sings and he bakes, and I watch him move through the bakery. I watch, then I'm helping. One day I sweep the walk while he finishes the baked apple tarts; another, I close the shop early so I can stop in at the bakery and repair a loose plug on the big oven. *We're friends*, I tell my wife when I'm spending more time at the bakery than I am at home and, *He doesn't have any family*, when she asks why he calls me every time something breaks. *I fix things*, I tell her. *I'm the guy who fixes things.*

You know he's a queer, she says, and I didn't, but *I don't care*, I say.

And I don't, but I do care that his face is soft, and his fingers are long, and his voice wraps around me like the first whispers of spring and the next time he calls me to fix something at the shop I ask if I can kiss him, and he says yes.

The Town Bakery

Raj hefts the specials board out to the sidewalk every morning at 6 AM. We filter in, looking for doughnuts or peanut butter cookies or those low-calorie banana nut muffins Mrs. Mansfield eats because she's on yet another diet. Sometimes, we even try the strange foreign desserts Raj sneaks onto the menu, like mango halwa and the sweet yellow squares with a name we can't pronounce. Raj sweeps the sidewalk before the sun comes up, washes the front windows, runs a rag over the handcarved wooden sign he ordered from Old Man Stephens when he first opened the shop last year.

We're lured in by the smell of cinnamon and brown sugar and the thick, sweet icing Raj pours onto his cinnamon buns without skimping and those luxurious petit fours he must spend hours decorating.

We tried to boycott the bakery after Raj seduced Barbara Stanley's husband and we succeeded for a while after John moved in and the two men sat at a table in the bakery, holding hands and looking inappropriately happy during down times. But Barbara kept going to work and doing her shopping and looking the same as ever and John kept fixing people's cars and Mrs. Mansfield complained that the banana nut muffins from the grocery store were dry and then we were eating at Raj's again, listening to his melodious whistles, and nothing had changed except now John Stanley was gay and Barbara wasn't his wife anymore.

Raj gave free warm cookies to the kids who came in with their parents and after a while, we stopped pulling them back when his hands reached to tousle their little heads. We almost loved him, Raj, loved the way he fed us and the way he whistled sections of Vivaldi's *Four Seasons* while he packed our goods into white paper bags.

After the robbery he closed for so long we wondered if he'd ever open again. We heard the assailant broke Raj's jaw in six places. He doesn't whistle anymore when he packs our cookies, but he still holds John's hand at a small table in the back during down times and the fresh coat of paint on the front of the shop has almost erased the memory of the spray-painted *faggot* we looked at every day while he was gone.

Sparrows Mate for Life

Betty Mansfield dabs her eyes with a cotton swab, leaving a swath of browns, peaches, and black across her lids. She glances in the mirror at Rob, sitting on the bed behind her. He's picking at his toenails, watching and talking, as he does every night. *Male sparrows have brown and black striping on their wings*, he says, and Betty stares down at the cotton. What if she kept rubbing? Wipe off the makeup, take off the epidermis and the next two layers of skin?

Birds only have two layers of skin, Rob tells her, they don't have sweat glands.

Betty imagines peeling all the fat from her body, peeling off her muscles and veins. Rob drones about the length of sparrows—14 to 18 centimetres—and Betty exposes a different person, someone who doesn't sit in front of the mirror every night listening to her husband talk about birds and dreaming about low-fat banana nut muffins and all the cookies she'd eat if she wasn't on a diet.

She lingers over her neck. Toner, then moisturizer. The turkey waddle is starting to appear in the sagging under her jawline. When she and Rob married, she'd been plump but firm. Now, she's soft all over and jiggly, despite months of dieting. She clenches her teeth, straining the neck muscles to tighten the skin.

Rob says birds don't have teeth, but she already knows that. Birds haven't had teeth in a hundred million years, even though they were descended from archosaurs which had teeth. Big ones, probably.

She bares her teeth in the mirror. How will Rob react if she strips off her extra layer of skin, if she grows wings, if she turns into a hawk and snatches his eyes from his face, bites off his fingers, leaves him howling as she flies into the night?

She puts down the towels and her makeup

sponges and joins Rob in bed. *Sparrows mate for life*, he says, as he rolls on top of her.

Poor things, Betty replies, but he isn't listening.

Painting the Walls of Raj's Tiny Room

John paints delphiniums on the wall behind the bed, dark blue to match Raj's tattoo. His hands, so steady when changing a serpentine belt or a spark plug, tremble as he draws his lover in purple. When Raj protests, John flicks paint at him. *Now you match.*

Raj steals the brush to paint stars in their eyes and moons across their chests. The smells of the bakery waft up from the shop below and the tiny studio apartment fills with cinnamon and maple and the smell of fresh-baked bread.

With a pencil from the nightstand, Raj draws a moustache on John's purple face, the one on the wall, and shrieks as bright blue handprints find his body. Up here, nothing exists—not the town, the bakery, the looks, not John's ex-wife, not even the attack that left Raj's mouth half-curled into a permanent smirk on one side. John's hands move along the wall, his fingertips swirling into pools of paint.

Dork, John scrawls above their portraits on the wall.

I love you, Raj writes with an arrow pointing to John.

John drops the brushes and pulls Raj close, his lips leaving a trail of little blue flowers that will never disappear.

Principal of the Year

Alan Farber shines his Principal of the Year trophy, surreptitiously watching Mrs. Stanley through the glass walls of his office as she rifles through her files with delicately manicured fingers. She's stunning today in a navy sweater set, dark stockings, and navy and white shoes with a slight but sensible heel. She looks up at him and smiles, but his head drops and he polishes the trophy with renewed fervour. "Barbara," he whispers to himself, preparing for the day he calls her by her first name. She won't be Mrs. Stanley for long, he tells himself, now that her husband is living with the man who runs the bakery. Alan plans on stepping up, offering comfort. Perhaps he'll bring her a cup of tea and ask her if she'd like to have dinner. His fingers linger on the cool silver-plated curves of the trophy as Mrs. Stanley turns from the file drawer and faces her computer. Maybe he should send her an email. He positions the trophy on the most visible spot on his desk, nudging it a little closer to the edge where Mrs. Stanley can't help but see it, then turns to his computer. *Dear Barbara*, he writes, tapping excitedly on the keys. The thrill of her first name coming from his own fingers. *Perhaps you would like to have dinner with me soon?* He imagines trying to find someone to come over and take care of his mother—or perhaps Mrs. Stanley would like to meet his mother, have dinner with them both, see the way he takes care of her now that she can no longer take care of herself. A tremor runs through his body at the idea of Mrs. Stanley rifling through his bookshelves the way she does with school files. She'd step in to help him get his mother to bed and after, come to him in the den where his rows of awards line the walls. *Oh, Alan*, she'd breathe, and his lips would smear her perfect lipstick.

I think we would have a lovely time. Warmest regards, Alan Farber.

He sends before he can lose his nerve and peers at her from around his desk as she looks at her computer. Her back stiffens and he ducks further down.

His notifications ping and he opens her email with trembling fingers.

Dear Mr. Farber, While I appreciate the invite, I prefer to keep our relationship professional. You are a very good boss and I'd hate to lose you. Sincerely, Mrs. Stanley.

You are a very good boss, he repeats, sliding his hands across the desk to snag his trophy. He cradles it in his arms and holds the cool metal to his flushed face. *I am a good boss*, he whispers into his trophy. His fingers caress the rounded shape of his pride and joy. *A very good boss.*

Always Hungry

My brother robbed a bakery. When I heard, I remembered him as a kid, always hungry, always demanding more food. I saw him running into the bakery, storming out with armloads of pastries, his face covered with powdered sugar. I almost laughed until they told me about the proprietor, his broken jaw and blackened eyes, the way my brother had spray-painted *faggot* on the front of the building after stealing from the cash register and leaving the owner for dead.

Always hungry, always demanding. That's how I remember him most, always wanting. After our father disappeared, when the money wasn't coming anymore at all, I'd serve him noodles and butter with salt and pepper and beg my mother to quit smoking so I could buy lunch meat and bread with the government money.

When we were teens, the church dropped off

a food box once a week—big blocks of cheese and a frozen chub of ground beef. I'd grill the beef until it was brown all the way through and slap it on a plate with yellow mustard and cheese. He was so skinny, my brother, even with all that church-issued food, and I was so fat, my body unable to process the constant diet of grease. I remember struggling to fit into my church dress for his first court appearance when we were still teens.

Make me a sandwich, Lana, he'd demand, always demanding. *Give me some cookies.* I'd hesitate, cookies in hand. They cost so much, more than we could afford on my mother's disability check. *Give me cookies*, he'd scream, near tears.

Just do it, my mother would snap from her almost permanent place at the kitchen table where she sat reading romance novels from the thrift store, losing herself in a world where men were strong and protective, and the women were always taken care of. I'd refresh her coffee again and again, sometimes lingering to catch a glimpse of words over her shoulder, blinking away from the smoke spiralling up from the cigarette in the thick snot-yellow ashtray my brother made in ceramics class.

Always hungry, I tell my wife after the bakery robbery, after my brother has been arrested and found guilty, and he begs me for money for a retrial, money we don't have because my wife's sister is dying and we're taking care of her children: Alistair, who is always hungry, and Kelvin, who never is.

I love you, I tell my brother through the plastic barrier at the prison. *I wish you the best.*

He stares at me in disbelief, stares because I never once told him no, not even once. He stares at me until we're both crying.

You have to get me out of here, he says.

I shake my head no. Our time is up, and I put my hand against the plastic, reaching for him, but he stands and moves away without turning back to look at me again, not even once.

Mr. Leopold Goes for a Run

On Tuesdays, Thursdays, and Sundays, we watch Mr. Leopold from our front rooms, from our windows. Him in his tiny running shorts and his awkward bounce-shuffle gait. He wheezes by Mrs. Stanley's and cuts into the alley. From here, most of us lose sight of him, but Betty Mansfield and her sister Cheryl, having coffee in Betty's mid-century modern tangerine kitchen, spot him darting around the trashcans in Old Man Havers's yard before he ducks into Eva Longing's side door.

Twenty-three minutes and he's out, panting and wheezing, cutting back around Old Man Havers's yard, jogging past Betty and Cheryl still lingering over their coffee. We watch him, hate him, but we don't talk about him because it's not our business and it's not like he's doing anything some of us haven't done before.

We peer from our windows and text each

other and he runs from Eva Longing, who works in the bakery and always has fresh-baked goods, back by Mrs. Stanley's house where she lives by herself because her husband left. Mr. Leopold runs into his own home where his wife makes him an omelette with extra cheese and a side of bacon because a man who runs as much as he does needs an awful lot of protein.

Alistair's Teacher

Alistair's teacher thanks me profusely for the cookies. Two dozen assorted, thoughtfully arranged in a white box. I thought Raj undercharged me for the cookies, but he swore he didn't. What do I know about the price of cookies? I don't eat them; I don't cook them. If Marian was still able to do things like bake, she'd be making cookies and bringing them to school. Raj's voice is careful and stilted when he speaks to me now and I don't know if it's because he knows it was my wife's brother who assaulted him or because he's being extra nice to me the way everyone has been extra nice since my sister started her long slow process of dying.

Even Brenda treats me carefully when she pops in to check Marian's vitals or make notes on the chart hanging at the end of the bed. Brenda and I had a three-week relationship a few years back that ended the day I met Lana, and Brenda still hasn't forgiven me for breaking up with her. But even she's extra nice now, gentle, as if being the loved one of the almost-dead elevates me from heartbreaker to pitiable stranger.

Alistair's teacher asks after Lana, asks if I have time to talk about Alistair's behaviour problems. I don't, not really, but I nod and then we're somehow sitting on opposite sides of her desk with this box of cookies between us and my ass spilling over a ridiculously small plastic chair that's the same colour of puke brown as the ones in Marian's room.

"He's doing fine," the teacher tells me, "considering the circumstances."

The circumstances happen to be lying in a hospital bed breathing with the help of a machine. I want to tell the teacher to give Alistair a break but I'm afraid of my rage, so I clench my teeth and swallow. When I can speak again, I ask, *What can we do to support him at this moment?* I want to pat myself on the back for sounding so compassionate yet professional, when really I want to shake Alistair for putting me in this situation.

He's just a child, Lana says every day when Alistair makes me angry in a new way. *A child,* I remind myself every time and part of me wants to hold him, to make this all make sense to him even though it doesn't make sense to me. The other part wants to scream at him, scream at my sister for leaving me to care for her kids when most days I can't take care of myself.

My Mother's Fingers

Mom's dying. No one says it aloud, but Kelvin told me we're going to live with Aunt Sal and Aunt Lana after, and he wouldn't say after what. Kelvin doesn't talk much at all, and he never eats, not even the cookies Aunt Sal brings from the bakery, the good ones with extra icing.

Aunt Sal's fingers clench and unclench in time to the machines keeping Mom alive. She used to come for whirlwind visits bringing gifts and telling stories with swear words that made my mom's mouth go tight. Aunt Sal used to laugh so loudly she'd snort and make me giggle even when I didn't get the joke. Now she's quiet, clenching her fingers, glaring at Kelvin who's tap tap tapping on the bedside table. She wouldn't notice if I got up and left, but maybe Mom would.

Kelvin won't talk to me. My mom can't. Aunt Sal doesn't say a word. She stares at Kelvin and he stares at the wall. My mom looks bruised and sad like the guy Aunt Lana's brother beat up. I've never been beat up, but Eric Nelson once kicked me in the crotch after I tagged him out and it hurt so bad I couldn't breathe. My mom can't breathe, not without that machine, that's what Kelvin told me. *We're going to live with our aunts*, Kelvin said. I don't want to live with them, though. Neither of them knows how to play video games or cook food I like to eat.

Aunt Sal's fingers keep moving the way my mom's fingers used to always move, always running along the pages of my favourite book as she read to me, moving over the controller when we played games together, moving through the dough when she made cookies for me and Kelvin. I want to reach for her still fingers now but instead, I pause and touch the machine attached to her bed, wishing they'd put me on it too, because right now, I can't breathe, not at all.

Mrs. Leopold's Cookies

"You never have to sit in a corner," my boss says for like the fifth time. He's been misquoting *Dirty Dancing* for about twenty minutes—even tried to get me to merengue with him when the line died down. I want to smack him, except the customer, who really does look exactly like Jennifer Grey pre-nose job, is sitting in the corner eating a cinnamon roll and every time I refill her coffee, her high-pitched voice surprises me, half-expecting as I am to hear Baby's smooth, deep tones.

"I'm waiting for my boyfriend," she tells me and I hate her for a moment for having a boyfriend she can see in public, like all the other couples who come into the bakery, like Raj, my boss, and John Stanley, his boyfriend, who hold hands at a back table every night at closing even though John used to be married to a woman who works at the high school and a lot of people took sides when they got divorced.

"How nice," I mutter as I pour the coffee. It is nice—nice for her to have a boyfriend who isn't married to someone else, who doesn't pretend not to know who she is when they run into each other in the grocery store.

Mrs. Leopold comes in for her daily dose of cookies and I step back, letting Raj rush behind the counter. He gushes over her clothing, her hair, the new perfume her sister sent her from a little boutique in New York City. She doesn't look my way and I want to step in front of her, let her see the differences between us, let her bask in my youth, the slender curves of my hips, the way my thrift store jeans hang just low enough to show brief glimpses of my perfectly flat belly.

Instead, I turn back to Baby and ask her where she met her boyfriend. Her eyes light up and the words fall from her mouth. Behind me, Raj slams the cash register and hands over Mrs. Leopold's cookies, cookies that will only make her fatter and less attractive.

"Do you have a boyfriend?" Baby asks me and I half-turn, watching Mrs. Leopold stride back across the bakery like a woman who has everything, and "No," I say, turning back to the girl who looks like Baby. "No, I don't."

A Pocketful of Cookies

The boy has, hidden in his pockets, several packages of stolen cookies. Not just any cookies, but soft oatmeal ones with thick squishy cream filling. He's so hungry he almost believes they'll taste of something other than cardboard or guilt. He also has, in his pockets, enough money to buy ten cookies, maybe twenty.

The cookies nestle against the money—money his Aunt Sal keeps pressing into his hands, little paper pieces of love that come easier than cooking a meal, easier than talking to him, easier than the ugly messiness of caring for a child who belongs to someone else.

Adam at the Table

Adam sits in the kitchen eating cookies. He looks the same as he always did—larger than life, blond, smiling. He shovels the cookies into his mouth by the handful, looking at me without a trace of rancour. "You never sent the cookies," he says, but his voice is warm, loving.

"I know." I slide into the chair opposite him. My hands ache to touch him but I can't. He disappears when I do. My skin is poison—it breaks the magic. "I'm so sorry," I whisper.

"I waited." He shrugs and his voice is sad, but he's still smiling, still my Adam, still my happy husband. He shoves another cookie into his mouth. "I told the guys you'd be sending them, told them my wife makes the best cookies in the world."

You shouldn't have counted on me, I want to say, but instead, I reach for him, drawn as I am every night to touch his skin, to make him understand. My fingers fall through nothing, and he's gone.

Free Cookies Taste Better

Kelvin upends a paper bag of oatmeal cookies on the counter and watches the clerk's eyes widen. She stares at him, mouth slightly gaped. Kelvin wants to laugh at her shock, wants to grab her and ask how she caught him stealing one lousy pack of cookies that he couldn't even eat when his little brother managed to shove a month's worth of cookies into his trousers and stroll out like he owned the place.

He knows she remembers him—he can tell. She must remember telling him to empty his pockets and finding the stolen goods among his piles of detritus. Her disappointment settles on his shoulders as she looks at the stolen cookies in front of her, perhaps remembering that she'd let him go with a warning, how she'd felt sorry for him, or that somehow, she knew that even stolen cookies made him choke, that even now he's afraid he'll never eat again without wanting to throw up.

But Alistair. Did he have to steal from the same store? Kelvin wants to go home and punch his brother.

My brother stole these, he wants to say. He doesn't tell the clerk that Alistair snuck out of the hospital and no one noticed because their dying mother stole everyone's ability to care about anything else. He doesn't tell her that Aunt Sal called the police, but Alistair got back before they showed up. He doesn't say that Aunt Sal didn't notice Alistair's bulging pockets and red-rimmed eyes because the moment he walked into the room, she snapped at Kelvin to keep a better eye on his brother before turning back to watch the machines keeping his mother alive.

He wants the clerk to yell at him. He wants her to call the police or ban him from the store or reach across the counter and clock him in the face. "I stole these right in front of your face," he says.

"I crammed them into my pockets, and you never saw me." He's waiting for the flash of anger, for the punishment he came here for.

Instead, the clerk steps around the counter and puts both hands on his forearm. Kelvin can't pull away, can't stop looking at her face. "All the cookies in the world won't fill that hole, kid," she says.

Crying now, Kelvin looks down at the clerk's hands, gently holding his arm. "What will?"

"I don't know," she whispers.

Kelvin wraps his arms around her and hugs her tight, tighter than he's hugged anyone since his mom got sick. When he releases her, she's crying, too.

"Go on, get out," she tells him, handing him one of the packets of cookies.

Kelvin pockets them and nods a goodbye. By the time he gets back to the hospital, he's ravenous.

Better than Homemade

Marjorie passes a cookie to her son. Chocolate chip, it used to be his favourite. Marjorie knew Bobby used to sneak over to Raj's bakery on his way home from school, using his allowance to purchase a cookie or two. On Bobby's tenth birthday, she'd bought dozens of cookies from Raj and took them to Bobby's class at school. Marjorie couldn't bake, but cookies from Raj were better than homemade. When Bobby enlisted, Raj gave him a free bag of cookies to take on the plane and when Marjorie broke her ankle and couldn't work, Raj and John Stanley, who used to be married to Barbara Stanley but is now in love with Raj, came over and cooked meals and cleaned Marjorie's house.

Bobby thought he was going to die. Marjorie saw it in his eyes when he told her he'd enlisted. She'd seen it in his shaking hands, in the rare letters he sent home, in the picture he sent of his best friend Adam, huge and golden next to her tiny, dark son.

She pushes the cookie to Bobby. Eat this, you used to love them.

He chokes on the first bite but clears his throat and keeps chewing. Marjorie notices Raj staring at them from behind the counter, concern on his face.

Bobby had a nervous breakdown, Marjorie has been told, and now she has to take him once a week to that shrink in the city. Marjorie browses the craft store while Bobby goes to his appointments. She'd bought enough yarn to make ten sweaters for those poor boys who just lost their mother, the ones who stole cookies from the shop, probably to feed the grief the way Marjorie keeps trying to feed her Bobby.

She passes him another cookie and he takes it. For a moment, their hands touch, and Marjorie squeezes his, wanting to pull him into her lap the way she'd done when he was little and came to her in tears after being pushed around by bullies.

I love you, she tries to say, but somehow, she can't squeeze the words past her lips and instead she says, *Have another cookie, son*, and he chews and cries as both their hearts break.

At Adam's House

My mom checks the GPS and pulls to the curb. "This is it," she says. She's forced this visit, spurred by my therapist who tells her it will help my mental state.

The house looks exactly like the pictures Adam used to show me—small and white with bright orange shutters because Adam loved cheerful. Two wooden rocking chairs cover half the front porch and for a moment I can see Adam and his wife sitting in them, sharing soft words and glasses of iced tea after putting their son to bed.

Why is the lawn so neatly trimmed? A flash of anger rips through my chest. The house looks perfect—not a broken toy on the grass or a lopsided shutter or a dangling porch light. "I don't want to do this."

My mom sighs and I can feel her checking off

an item on her laundry list of things to do to make Bobby less crazy. She pushes my shoulder. "Just go knock on the door."

"You're not coming with me?" I don't want her to come, but I don't want to go alone. My therapist says this is an important part of my healing, meeting Adam's wife. But I suddenly hate her, hate that the tidy house and lawn show no sign of his absence.

My mom leans back in her seat and pulls out a paperback. She's not going anywhere. She's been navigating my return to mental health like a gym teacher with a whistle. Homemade chicken noodle soup. Check. Weekly therapy visits. Check. Drive Bobby to see the wife of his dead best friend. Check.

"I have to do this on my own time," I tell her, but she doesn't look up from her book. I slam the car door behind me and stalk to the front door. *Why are you okay?* I plan to scream at Adam's wife.

Who's mowing the lawn?

Adam's wife opens the door before I can knock. She looks at me without speaking and my anger dissipates under her gaze. She isn't as tidy as the house and lawn, with dark circles under her eyes and a tightness around her mouth. *I can still feel his guts sliding down my face*, I want to tell her. *I wash him off me a dozen times a day.*

She holds out her hand and I take it. "I had a nervous breakdown," I say, holding her hand. "After he died."

"I sent the cookies too late," she says. "I kept putting it off. I thought I had time."

"He stepped on a mine. He exploded."

Her hands squeeze mine hard enough to hurt. "A routine patrol. That's what they told me."

We're holding hands and then she steps into my arms and we're both crying. "He loved you," she says. I'm supposed to be comforting her but all I can remember is Adam and the cookies that came too late. "I ate them," I gasp between sobs. "The cookies you sent."

"I sent them to you since I couldn't send them to him," she says.

She's crying and she mutters against my neck, and I think she's saying something about how her son, Adam's son, mows the lawn now just like his dad and for the first time, I can't feel Adam's guts dripping down my face. I pull away. "He loved you," I say, holding her arms to make sure she understands what I'm saying. "His eyes. They did this thing when he talked about you."

"Would you like to come in? I'd like you to meet my son." She smiles for a moment. "I have some fresh-baked cookies."

I glance back at the car. My mom, pretending not to watch, holds her book in front of her face. I turn back to Adam's wife. "Is it okay if I invite my mom?"

This Girl

The neighbours flip through Anna's life like browsers at a garage sale. Flip, her weight. Flip, her bad perm. Flip, her long hours teaching and designing lesson plans. Flip, her volunteer hours at the literacy project. Flip, her bad cooking. *You can't really blame him*, some of them say. *A man has needs*, others whisper.

She stalks into the bakery, ignoring Raj who rushes to the counter as usual. "My gorgeous love," he says, but she keeps walking, veering to the middle of the room where Eva Longing waits tables in low-slung jeans and a half-top.

From the corner of her eye, Anna catches Brenda waving, but Anna ignores her. Brenda came to school to talk about nursing on career day. After, she'd pulled Anna aside. *I should tell you this since no one else will.*

No one should tell anyone anything, Anna thinks.

She stops in front of Eva who squares her shoulders and faces Anna. *This girl*, Anna thinks. *This girl.* The girl trembles but her face is set. This girl who's ready to fight for Anna's skinny husband, ready to go to battle over a man who chews his own toenails and won't eat bananas until they're almost black. This girl who has no idea about hard backs turned into silence and long nights of resentment and the comfort of knowing it may not be wonderful but at least it's familiar.

This girl, Anna thinks. She stares at the young woman for a few moments. "You win," she says. She strides out of the bakery, swinging her purse. Outside, she smiles. "You win." She laughs. "Good luck with that."

Cigarettes and a Flowered Housedress

Grandma Jane oozes from the side wall and slips into the chair Sal had been sitting in an hour ago. "She's finally gone," Grandma says. She never cared for Sal, not like she cared for me. Homophobic, our Gran, with a side of racism to boot. When we were in college, Sal came home with her first girlfriend, a dark-haired woman named Renney who stared Grandma down when she asked where Renney was from and Renney said, "Nelson."

Grandma Jane wears a violet and orange flowered housedress, a polyester button-front number with giant pockets stuffed with packs of cigarettes, tissues, a TV remote, and a bag of dog treats. She was always feeding that little dog of hers, feeding it until it was rounder than it was tall, fed it to death, really, and it died three months before she did.

"Ah fuck," Grandma says, which was the second-to-last thing she said before she died. "Marian, I did my best," was the last, and I don't know if Sal ever forgave me for being the last thing on Grandma's mind when she went. Sal hated Gran, loved her, too, as people do when they're raised under a cloud of disappointment and anger. "Didn't think you'd be here this soon," Grandma continues, patting around for a pack of cigarettes. She lights one and blows smoke from the corner of her mouth. I roll my eyes to the smoke alarm above her head, praying she doesn't bring the force of an army of nurses down on me.

"Is this it? I'm going out and you're the loving relative sent to guide me home?"

"I always loved you," she says from behind a cloud of smoke rings. "Did my best by you, too."

"Not by Sal."

"No, not Sal," she admitted. "Never could understand that child." She reaches in her pocket again and the dress shifts or changes colour and it's the same one I remember her wearing the day she died, the day Sal and I found her on the kitchen floor, a cigarette bent under her, and "Ah fuck," she'd said when we rolled her over.

I struggle to sit up, but my lungs aren't cooperating, and the movement makes it hard to breathe. Gran watches as I collapse back on the pillows, panting. It should have been my mom sitting here with me or my dad, who tried, in his way, to be a devoted father even after the divorce. My former husband could have seen me home, or his parents who, from the first time Harry brought me to meet them, treated me like the daughter they never had. I stare at my grandma and count the dead souls in my life. Three miscarriages, my younger brother, my boss from the library. I'm joining them and she's the one they sent. I'm filled with such a wave of rage that the force of it drives me from my bed. My hands flail for the side table and I knock over vases of flowers and boxes of cookies, piles of presents, and cards and letters.

Leaning over her, shaking with anger. "I hated you," I tell her. "Hated how you treated Sal. Hated how you drove a wedge between us by favouring me."

Her mouth drops open and I laugh, a breathless, painful laugh. "Sal was better than me," I tell her. "Better than you." God, how Sal and I had hated each other for so long after we escaped from Gran, how we'd believed the things she'd thought about us for so long. Sal, who sits at my bedside daily, who takes care of my boys, who finally went home to get a couple hours of sleep and who will probably carry the guilt of not being here when I died, for the rest of her life. My hands tremble as I reach out, to take her cigarette, to slap her, I don't know, but she's gone, and my movement throws me off balance. I land on the floor on my hands and knees in the piles of gifts. I pick at one of the cards, a thick cream-coloured one with a bear on the front. *Get Well Soon* it says in cheerful hopelessness. I clutch it to my chest and pray that a nurse finds me before Sal comes back with my boys.

My Sister's Life

I leave my home and end up somewhere else. Rows of manicured lawns, white fences, faces pretending not to stare as the moving truck pulls up in front of what used to be my sister's house and will now be my new home.

It makes more sense for me and Lana to move into Marian's home. More sense not to uproot the boys from their schools, their friends. Here, breathing in Marian's scent, touching her clothes, pulling out the rows and rows of cookie sheets, I almost can't believe she's gone.

Lana directs the movers to put our stuff in the guest bedroom; we can't bring ourselves to sleep in Marian's room.

I leave my apartment and end up as the head of my sister's house, feeding her children, tiptoeing into their rooms at night to see if they're sleeping.

After, Lana and I lie next to each other,

breathing softly. She doesn't speak and I know she's wondering what this new life means for us, wondering how we go from drag queen bingo, lesbian potlucks, concerts, parties, and late-night takeout eaten naked in bed, to a life of cooking for children, making cookies for bake sales, and going to parent-teacher conferences.

Alistair cries out and I rush to his room to wipe his flushed face and murmur sleepily until he falls back asleep. In the hallway, I step on a toy car and bite my lip to keep from crying out because if I start crying, I'm not ever going to stop and for a moment, I hate Marian for leaving me with these boys, boys who used to see me as the favourite aunt, and who see me now as not-their-mom.

I limp back to bed and Lana's arms open automatically. She tucks against my shoulder, her short, soft hair tickling my chin. As I'm drifting back to sleep, I'm sure I hear her murmur, "For better or worse, my love."

Kelvin Comes Home

Kelvin sweeps into the house carrying a duffle bag of laundry and a box of Raj's cookies. "I stopped on the way in," he says in the new deep voice he's developed in his first year at college. Alistair screeches into the room, throwing himself at his older brother. He's almost as tall as Kelvin now, almost as grown up. Aunt Sal waits behind Alistair, letting the brothers have their moment before she steps up and relieves Kelvin of the cookies, pressing her cheek for a moment to his slender face.

"You're so thin," she tells him. "We'll eat dinner as soon as Lana gets home from work."

Kelvin rolls his eyes but he's happy for the attention, happy because he knows Lana will cook luscious meals for the next week and he'll go back to school feeling nurtured and loved.

Kelvin untangles himself from Alistair, whose

hair is getting so long, and readjusts his duffle on his shoulder. In his room, he drops the bag and stares around at the place he still calls home, though it looks like someone else's room now. He runs his fingers over superhero posters, missing Spiderman who he guesses he'll find in Alistair's room.

In a few minutes, he'll go to the kitchen and share Raj's cookies with his aunts and his brother, and they'll reminisce about the years they've spent in this house. They'll talk about his mother because they can now, they can say her name even without anger and guilt and the weight of everything they lost when she died.

And even later, maybe Kelvin will visit Bobby's mom who once caught him stealing and didn't call the police, who has knit him a sweater every year since his mom died, who used to come over on the weekends and patiently learn from Aunt Lana how to bake cookies, while Bobby, who was older than Kelvin and much cooler, would talk to the younger boys as if they weren't delicate orphans but regular boys who liked snakes and cars and trying on Bobby's army jacket. And maybe Bobby's mom will say Bobby had asked about him, had heard that Kelvin still sometimes visits Josh Parker, the boy who lost his dad a few years ago because Kelvin wants to be to Josh what Bobby was to him.

Alistair ducks into Kelvin's room and perches on the bed. "I'm glad you're home," he says.

Kelvin gently tugs a lock of his brother's hair. "When did this get so long?"

Alistair looks away, looks at the posters. "I took Spiderman."

"I figured."

"Aunt Sal says to wash up and come to dinner," Alistair says without making a move to get up.

Kelvin flops next to Alistair. "How's everything here?"

Alistair clenches and unclenches his fingers. "I'm in trouble at school."

"Again?"

"Yeah."

Kelvin waits. He'd kept his own head down through most of high school, but it was no sense telling Alistair to do the same. Alistair who wears glittery t-shirts and tight plaid pants and who experiments with eyeliner and styling his hair in a way that makes Aunt Sal and Aunt Lana laugh and look for old music videos from the 80s on YouTube. "Everything comes back," one of them always says. "Nothing ever goes away forever."

Alistair says, "I think I might be gay."

We know, Kelvin wants to say. Instead, he puts his arm around his younger brother and tries to think of how to tell him not to add one more target to himself, to hide it until he's out of school, to think of how people still call Lana Aunt Sal's "friend" though they've been together fifteen years, or about the time someone beat up Raj at the bakery after he fell in love with John Stanley, or about that kid from Kelvin's class who committed suicide, but he can't because it's Alistair and if there's one thing Kelvin learned from hating himself most of his life it's that you have to at least be real, if you can't be happy. He hugs Alistair even tighter and says, "That explains your wardrobe."

Alistair snorts and punches Kelvin on the arm.

The two boys traipse to the kitchen, arms slung around each other, to share some cookies with their family.

The Feather He Brings

Ari brings me a feather. It trembles between his fingers, and I can almost see a bubble hanging over his head, a question, a glimmer of hope.

"Alistair," he says, and I want to respond but my knees have turned inward, and I lean against the door frame, putting space between our bodies.

There's no air between us, just silence and this feather, and Ari's unspoken question hanging in the thought bubble over his head and me leaning against the door, afraid of his vulnerability, terrified I'm going to pop that bubble and ruin him forever.

The silence between us gushes, a waterfall of nothing, and Ari's fingers tremble. *We can't do this*, I want to say to this boy who sits next to me in chemistry class, who brings homemade brownies from home and shares them with me every day. *Keep your head down*, my brother would say, but Ari's face is soft and so close.

The feather shifts in his grip and falls, clinging to the giraffe on the front of his shirt. For a moment, it looks as if the giraffe has a moustache and I bite my lip to keep from laughing. Instead, I brush the feather from Ari's shirt. His fingers come up to my tie, spiralling around the patterns and I close my eyes, close my throat, close everything inside of me that wants to crush him to me, tell him it doesn't matter that we're both boys, tell him he'll never have to chase me again because I've stopped running and for a moment, the question is answered even though he never asked.

Back in the Bakery

Every morning at 6 AM, John Stanley hefts the specials board out to the sidewalk. We straggle in all morning, looking for cookies and pies. Lottie Mansfield still eats those low-calorie banana nut muffins every day even though Mr. Mansfield lost his job at the post office and Lottie had to pick up work at the thrift store across from the middle school.

Raj doesn't sneak those strange foreign desserts onto the menu anymore and sometimes we miss them, those sweet yellow squares and the mango halwa. John Stanley sweeps the walk and washes the front windows while Raj bakes and hands out our cakes and brownies and the town's latest obsession: apple fritters.

Raj and John Stanley don't touch in public, but their eyes meet over our heads and Raj gives that sad little crooked smile he's had since getting beat up in the robbery. Sometimes, John Stanley's ex-wife even comes in and everyone gets quiet as she buys cinnamon rolls and smiles with her teeth clenched and John Stanley says hello in a hearty voice that echoes around the shop.

Marian's boys, who are practically grown, sit at a table in the front, drinking free hot chocolate, in oversized handmade sweaters that the clerk from the convenience store has made for them every year since their mom died of cancer. We lean in to listen when their Aunt Sal, who has cares for them since their mother died, whispers to say thank you to Raj, but Kelvin, who's home from college with the news that he's moved in with his girlfriend, has already thanked Raj, thanked him and hugged him, even asked about the wedding to John Stanley and if many of their friends from the town came.

The smell of apples waft out of the bakery, across the street, even down as far as the school and we're drawn in because we must know what

Raj is doing next, what fall treats he might display. Even the clerk from the convenience store comes in with her adult son Bobby who once had a nervous breakdown but now works at the insurance company and tries to sell us insurance when we see him in the street.

And Bobby sees the boys and talks to them with the ease of someone who has also faced grief and handled it poorly. The younger boys laugh under his gentle teasing and Kelvin, who used to be so skinny before he went to college, takes a bite of the cookies his aunt bought from Raj.

Their Aunt Sal turns her eyes to the clerk and thanks her again for the sweaters and the clerk asks after Aunt Sal's wife. And we're not surprised when the aunt reaches for the clerk and takes her hand like you'd hold on to your mother and says, *I still feel like I'm doing everything wrong,* and the clerk says, *All of us do, love. All of us always do.*

Acknowledgements

This collection wouldn't exist without Jude Higgins, who ran the class in which I wrote the first piece, and Sara Hills, who read that story and said, "I'd read a whole novel about these characters."

I'd also love to thank:

The entire team at Off Topic Publishing, especially founding editor Marion Lougheed who not only insisted my work was worth publishing, but who also somehow managed to convince me.

My incredible wife, August van Stralen, who is my first reader, my best friend, and eternally patient when I disappear for long hours to sit at my desk drinking copious amounts of Murchie's orange spice tea, staring out the window, and randomly swearing at my computer screen.

The writers' lifeline group—you know who you are—for always being willing to read and commiserate with a private message rage rant.

Andrew Buckley, who always brings me back to happy, even when I'm deeply entrenched in writing about trauma.

Andrew Shaughnessy, who is my go-to beta reader and who always manages to make my work better than it has a right to be.

Special thanks to the Bath Flash Fiction Awards for publishing "The Cookies Adam Couldn't Eat" in their award anthology *Snow Crow*.

Bonus Content

A Note From Finnian

I'm a fan of deep stories. Heartbreaking stories. Stories that make you cry or think or both—hopefully. I like to read and write stories that leave readers questioning life, struggling to find answers, digging into their own assumptions. And yet...

Sometimes a story is just entertainment. In the following bonus material, I've included quirky, funny, or just plain odd stories. Consider it my light-hearted offering to the weird place inside of you that longs for silliness. Consider it my concession to the fact that not everything has to be serious, that we can acknowledge the infinite heartbreak of the human experience and then raise our middle fingers to it.

Consider it an expression of my gratitude to

you for taking the journey with me, even when it was hard.

    Love,
    Finn

My Office Window

My neighbour runs to take out the garbage in droopy white underwear. The wind sends a plastic grocery bag dancing into the street. He pounces and catches it, bending over to pick up an errant piece of trash. Fabric shifts, flesh appears. Clearly visible private parts hang from the seams. There's an invisible line on his thermometer that determines if he'll put clothing on before taking out the trash. From my desk, I watch him drag the cans while I listen to the weather forecast, hoping for a cold front, a snowstorm, anything. Dear God, please let winter stick around.

The Day the Ants Took Over Forever

Kids in tight pants dancing through my store. Even the boys are wearing makeup, great smears of yellow and blue eyeshadow and ruffled shirts. Am I getting old or do kids today all look alike?

Talk about Ant Music, one of the kids says to me. *Dooby dooby doo wop*, another sings. They all laugh, spin around each other and I'm afraid, afraid of where this country is going, afraid of this modern music, this Ant Music that means nothing to me but apparently spurts teens to dress like Henry the Eighth's court got lost in Sephora.

They stream to the counter, in pairs, in trios, or groups, buying candy and sodas and they're laughing, singing, hugging, and dancing. More stream in, jostling the early ones. For a moment, I can't breathe in this vision of an army of gender-bending teenagers taking over the world with music and makeup and *Hey, man, it's 1985*, one of the kids says to me. *Lighten up*.

And a hush falls over the crowd and they part en masse and then he's walking toward me, a cross-dressing pirate with giant hoop earrings. *I'm Adam*, he tells me, and *these are my ants.*

This is our world now, someone whispers and I hand over the snacks and the money in the register and they stream from my store on their way to take over the world and in their absence, I lock the doors, turn off the lights, and go in the back to rummage through my Beatles records and restore my normalcy.

Denture Man and Hot Dog Mo

Johnna steps out onto her porch as I'm rushing by her house and looks at me as if I'm weird, but she's wearing her housecoat in the pouring rain, drinking coffee from a teacup so she doesn't have room to talk. I'm race-walking home, both the cat and I miserably blinking against the pouring rain, caught woefully unprepared for the sudden winter rainstorm. And there's Johnna all *Never seen a cat in a stroller.*

Fifty more steps and I would have made it and instead Johnna's waving me to stop because she has leftover marrow and thinks I should take it home to my wife. I'm trying to absorb the concept of leftover marrow when Denture Man and Hot Dog Mo turn the corner. These are the people (and dogs) in my neighborhood. Denture Man smiles wider and wider as he gets closer.

Denture Man sings "Circles in the Sand" in a mezzo-soprano, serenading me or perhaps Johnna, while Hot Dog Mo sniffs at my cat, unsure perhaps of the packaging, unfamiliar perhaps with the concept of a stroller.

"Stand down, Mo," Denture Man says, flicking his bridge in and out of his mouth with his tongue.

Johnna pulls a raw hot dog from the pocket of her housecoat. "Want a hot dog, Mo? Want a hot dog?"

"Don't give him a hot dog, he'll fart all night," Denture man says, but the hot dog is already flying through the air and Mo catches it midflight. My wife says the word *surreal* was invented in 1937, but it's been perfected here in 2021 outside my house.

Denture Man yells at Johnna, something about hot dogs and diarrhea, but I'm already escaping as they argue so I miss the rest. As I'm hoisting the stroller up the front stairs, Johnna yells, "What about the marrow?"

I scream back, "I'm a vegetarian!" before slipping through the door.

Kanga Catches a Break

Kanga Mills punches a middle manager in the break room. We're at the coffee bar, high-dosing caffeine to get through the McMaster project.

Kanga has been called Kanga since Scotty from accounting referred to him that way after Mills jumped from his third-floor office window while his bewildered secretary gaped and screamed behind him. When Kanga came back to work, he remained Kanga despite strongly worded memos from human resources asking people to lay off it.

Middle-Manager's hands clasp over his nose, blood spurting between his fingers. His shock of orange hair trembles around his head as he sobs and shakes. Cara, who's new enough not to hate anyone, not even middle management, grabs paper towels and holds them to the poor guy's nose, *shhhshhhshhh*, hushing him as you would a crying child.

I worked on that project for months, Kanga says,

about the project that won an award for the company, the project that got Andy promoted to the fifth floor. Kanga's face crumples from rage to bewilderment and even Andy has the sense to look abashed.

We watch for a few minutes as Cara comforts the suit and security comes to escort Kanga to his office with the brand-new windows so he can collect his things and go home and drink a whiskey.

And maybe, tomorrow, when Kanga is applying for unemployment and we're back to the McMaster project, we'll drink too much coffee and talk about how Kanga Mills escaped in the only way you can, if you're not willing to jump from a higher floor.

Wolf and the Redhead

It wasn't the disaster we'd made it out to be, what happened to Wolf. After all, it's not like he had done anything the rest of us hadn't. Fallen in love with a small town, opened a business, joined the committee for the kids' Olympics. We weren't even surprised when Wolf came over all heart and kindness with a tray of brownies for Grandma Joan over on Baker Street, after the dementia diagnosis and then bladder cancer and all she wanted to eat was chocolate and the great man obliged, telling her kids that when he's 98 if all he wants to eat is chocolate, apocalypse be damned, he's eating chocolate.

Wolf's lost some teeth since moving in and though some say he's better for it, some say he's been wearing Grandma's night gown and sleep hat lately in the evenings and snarling at the redheaded granddaughter of hers who likes to show up with thick and gooey recovery drinks, for

Grandma's health, she says. And the hippies next door suggested baking some pot into those brownies, because after all, Grandma isn't getting any younger and a paper-thin slice of the devil's weed might help her journey to heaven.

But Red says no and purses her lips and Wolf's smile sinks and dies before it even sets sail and Wolf starts remembering how he once trained for the London Olympics instead of baking brownies for a dying old woman with a sharp-tongued granddaughter. Escape dances in his eyes, escape from us, from this town, from the bar, from the kids and their needs and the sick old woman and for a minute, we can see the beast in the man, the leaping, snarling creature who came to town decades ago, and he's almost gone, almost out the door but then, "Could you go to the pharmacy to pick up Grandma's pills?" the redhead says, batting her eyelashes, and Wolf's moment is gone.

Great-Great-Grandpa's Teeth

George Washington didn't really have wooden teeth, but my great-great-grandfather did, and they grin at me from the dresser, the kitchen table, the mantle, or wherever I've moved them, looking for that special spot where they won't creep me out.

But *They're all we have left*, my mother said, crying, when she gave them to me shortly after the birth of my first child. *It's tradition*, she said, and *Someday, you'll pass them on to your oldest when they have their first child.*

Great- great-grandpa's teeth click when I walk past. I tried to hide them in a closet but then I dreamed about them, giant chomping wooden teeth chasing me through the hallways of my house.

Just get rid of them, my husband grumbles periodically, but I can't—we all know what happened when my mom's mom tried to throw them away, how a howling laugh followed as she ran from the garbage, how she fell and sprained her ankle, how she cried as she crawled back to the trash can to retrieve the teeth, how sometimes, even now, far into her old age, she whispers *I'm sorry, I'm sorry* whenever someone mentions teeth.

So they sit and watch and sometimes they chatter, and I lie awake in bed at night praying and praying for the birth of my first grandchild.

Mannequin Body Parts

Alfred, that's the man's name. The one who cleans up after the others go home. He shuffles through the dark storeroom, green coverall zipped up to the neck, push broom making a slow, steady path in front of him. "Hi Betty," he says to an arm twisted over the edge of a mail cart. "There ya are, Shelley," he calls to a pair of plastic legs shoved behind a pile of cardboard boxes.

We don't talk to him, this Alfred, this cheery man with a wide grin and ruddy cheeks, but we listen and he tells us about his day, how his wife came through cataract surgery just plumb fine, thank you Lord, and his newest grandchild just learned to say popcorn.

"Ah, Raylene," he says, as he lifts a sawed-off torso from the cold tile floor and places it on the shelf next to an orange-haired head with darkly painted crimson lips. We don't know how he knows our names when we don't even know them ourselves, but they always sound right. One plastic pile of body parts becomes Norma, another Jennifer.

"Oh, Martha," Alfred says, his voice deep with emotion. "What have they done to ya." His hands cradle the snapped-off fingers, sort them into their proper order, find the hand they belong to. "They don't mean to hurt ya, ladies," Alfred says. "They just don't know."

"My gout is acting up something fierce," he says, as he eases a headless body back onto a shelf. He lumbers around the room, looking for her head perhaps, but a stock boy kicked it under a shelf earlier in the day and it's buried in the dust now, staring for eternity at the moldy baseboards in the corner of the room. "I'm sorry, Candice," he says, and he covers her headless body with a cloth.

We're silent for a moment. We're always silent but it's deeper, more fraught as we stare at the walls, the ceiling, the floor, each other—wherever they've thrown our heads, wherever our gazes have landed. Our sprawled collection of breasts and limbs and necks and hands breathe in silence for Candice and secretly wish we'd been the ones to go into the forever unconscious.

"Well, here you are," Alfred calls, and he unearths Candice's unblinking head from under the shelf, reattaches her head. "It's a good day," he says, smiling, now whistling, and he gently turns her head so her face aligns with her body. "There's life in the old girl yet." He eases her into a stand, arms and legs and head and face, ready to be used, and unblinking eyes, deadened, hollow unblinking eyes that never ever get to cry.

Francis Becomes Disillusioned at Rodeo-Clown School

Francis digs and digs his fingernails into the desk, slowly carving his name into the pockmarked wood. Theory is so boring. When he signed up for rodeo-clown school, he'd had such high hopes of a life of excitement and glamour. Women, free drugs, scads of money raining on him as crowds cheered. And here again, he's working on an essay: "How to Ameliorate the Symptoms of Lower Back Trauma on the Rodeo Circuit." In front of him, Clark Tucker juggles wadded-up balls of paper whenever the teacher turns his back. The class clown at clown school. What a joke.

Francis moved to Nacogdoches for fame and fortune. But his father had warned him to study hard and pay attention, not to get swept up in the glitter and gluttony of the wild life. As the teacher lectures on about the importance of accurate APA citations, Francis's feet start tapping. The circuit calls him. He tries to focus on the teacher's words, but the call is too loud.

In the distance, he hears hollers and a *hoo howdy, my son*. A brigade of clowns, brightly coloured noses and wigs shining in the noonday sun, rips past the window, throwing up great clouds of dirt.

Francis looks back to the teacher one more time, his father's words of caution echoing in his head. He slowly rips up his essay, before tossing down his pen and rushing after his people.

About the Author

Finnian Burnett holds a doctoral degree in English pedagogy and teaches undergrad creative writing and English. Their writing explores intersections of identity—fatness, mental health, disability, queer joy. Finnian was a finalist for the 2023 CBC Nonfiction Prize. Their work has appeared in *Blank Spaces Magazine*, *Wordworks*, *Pulp Literature*, *Reflex Press*, and more. Their first novella-in-flash, *The Clothes Make the Man*, is available through Ad Hoc Fiction. Finnian received a Canada Council for the Arts grant to expand that collection into a novel. Finnian lives in British Columbia where they spend their time watching a lot of *Star Trek* and daydreaming about teleportation. Find them at www.finnburnett.com

More Books from Off Topic Publishing

All titles available at

offtopicpublishing.com/shop

or from your usual ebook vendors

All Forgotten Now, by Jennifer Mariani

In these poems, Jennifer Mariani grieves a life she can't return to, as she struggles to belong elsewhere. This work explores the reality of growing up white in post-independence Zimbabwe: Jennifer's own privilege juxtaposed with everyday poverty and racism. The poems in this book cry out with grief and rage and loss, and sometimes celebration. Every page is warm with the heat of Africa and wet with the tears of unbelonging.

"[A] stirring collection." - Yejide Kilanko, bestselling author of *Daughters Who Walk This Path* and *A Good Name*

Wayward & Upward: Stories & Poems

A woman runs from a cult leader.

A man watches a crowd carry a baby into the woods.

A boy makes a childhood friend who is much older than she appears.

The forty pieces in this book unite two creative endeavours at the heart of humanity: making music and telling stories.

"Metafictional conversations and stand-alone pieces alike shine with creativity, taking thought experiments to a whole other level of engagement." - Michelle Butler Hallett, Winner of the Thomas Raddall Atlantic Fiction Prize, *Constant Nobody*

Wanderers:
Poems From Those Who Cross Borders

Whether seeking asylum, travelling between homes, or studying abroad, these poems shimmer and roar with the chaos, beauty and astonishment that come with crossing borders. The impetus for crossing varies, but whatever the reason, borders loom large in the lives of these poets.

"Everyone's experience of borders is different, and beautiful. Read this book." - Mary Grace van der Kroef, author of *The Branch That I Am*

Exhaustion: Limited Reserves

Used up or worn out. Reaching the limits of our personal and collective resources. Laying waste to the planet. Burning fuel until there's nothing left but fumes. Each story and poem in this book engages exhaustion anew, revealing human struggles, moments of grace, and a relentless questioning.

"Society pressures us to carry stress, even when it weighs more than we do. These pieces reflect that common experience and give words to the silent struggles that isolate us within ourselves." - Renee Cronley, nurse and author of *Burnout*

Home: An Anthology

What is home? Is it a place? A feeling? A person? Does it shift and change? Can you point towards it but never quite attain it? Through poems and flash fiction from diverse voices, this anthology wrestles with the complexities of belonging.

"The voice came again. "You are welcome here, Jia, if you are as committed to peace as you claim. Come and take refuge." - from "Refuge" by Dawn Vogel (short story in *Home*)

Standing Up: A Charity Anthology for Ukraine

You rose up: against tyranny, convention, rudeness, unfavourable odds, malevolence, apathy. Against your boss, your barista, your worst enemy, your best friend, yourself. You saved the day. Actually, maybe made things worse. Made a difference. Got flattened. Did it work? Well, life's complicated. But one thing's for sure: On that day, you saw something you believed was wrong and you took action.

This anthology's proceeds will be 100% donated to the Canada-Ukraine Foundation.